No Accident

by

Lesley Howarth

Illustrated by Kirstin Holbrow

First published in Great Britain by Barrington Stoke Ltd
10 Belford Terrace, Edinburgh, EH4 3DQ

ISBN 1-902260-45-7
Printed by Polestar AUP Aberdeen Ltd

MEET THE AUTHOR - LESLEY HOWARTH

What is your favourite animal?
A rabbit
What is your favourite boy's name?
Jack
What is your favourite girl's name?
Georgia
What is your favourite food?
Curry
What is your favourite music?
Chart music
What is your favourite hobby?
Coast path walking

MEET THE ILLUSTRATOR - KIRSTIN HOLBROW

What is your favourite animal?
My dog, Pewter Plum
What is your favourite boy's name?
George
What is your favourite girl's name?
Beryl
What is your favourite food?
Shellfish
What is your favourite music?
Ambient techno
What is your favourite hobby?
Rowing on the River Wye

Barrington Stoke was a famous and much-loved story-teller. He travelled from village to village carrying a lantern to light his way. He arrived as it grew dark and when the young boys and girls of the village saw the glow of his lantern, they hurried to the central meeting place. They were full of excitement and expectation, for his stories were always wonderful.

Then Barrington Stoke set down his lantern. In the flickering light the listeners were enthralled by his tales of adventure, horror and mystery. He knew exactly what they liked best and he loved telling a good story. And another. And then another. When the lantern burned low and dawn was nearly breaking, he slipped away. He was gone by morning, only to appear the next day in some other village to tell the next story.

Contents

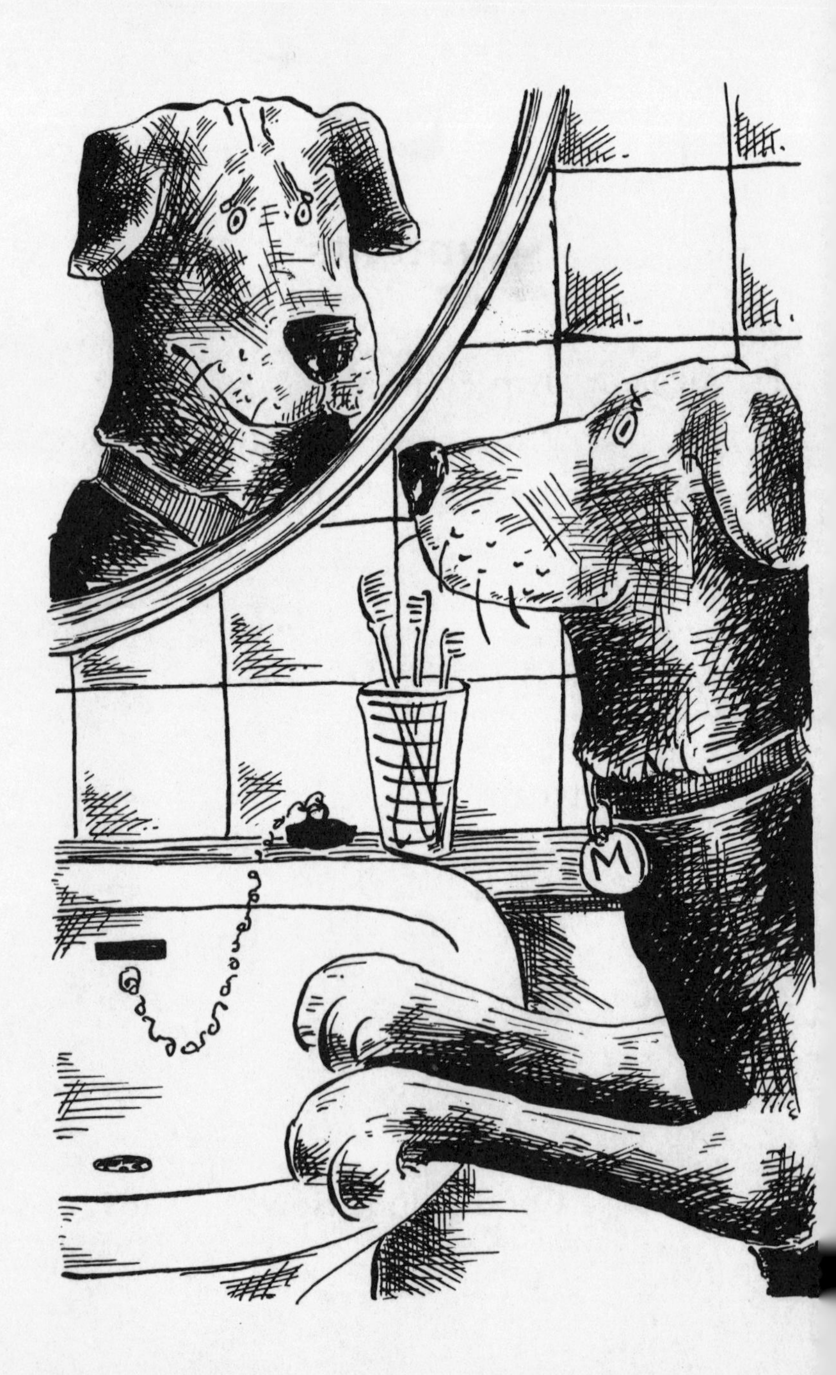

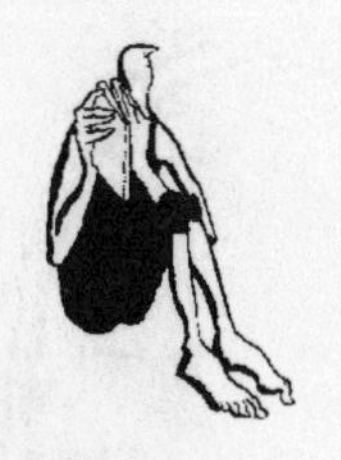

Chapter 1
All Your Own Fault

Milo barged into the bathroom. He looked into the mirror at the same time as a large, floppy black Labrador looked out of it. Milo had seen this Labrador before. It tried to sniff at him whenever he put his nose anywhere near the glass.

It didn't matter to Milo that he wasn't allowed in the bathroom. Someone had

forgotten to shut the door properly behind them. So in he went.

The hissing sound that very often came from behind the curtain told Milo that it was raining in there. Sometimes people came and stood in the rain behind the curtain. Very often it was Joe.

Clothes lay over the towel rail. Milo sniffed them. They smelled of Joe. He lapped up some water on the tiles.

"Milo?" Joe said. "That you?"

Milo put his paws on the toilet. Then he humphed down again. He wagged his tail against the shower curtain.

"Milo," Joe said. "Go out."

But Milo didn't go out.

Instead he ate Joe's watch. The shiny thing with the crunchy strap went down very nicely. If only Joe hadn't stepped out of the shower in time to see it go down ...

"Milo!" Joe smacked Milo's nose. Milo sneezed. But still the watch stayed down. "Milo! I don't believe you! What have you *done!*"

Milo was always swallowing things. The vet had x-rayed him several times already and had removed a cork from his insides. Also, he'd sicked up a lot of rubber matting last year. Milo, that is, not the vet.

Other things Milo had swallowed included *Get Down and Dance: Summer Groove Mix*. The tape had unwound in his stomach and had been expensive to remove. He also swallowed potatoes, as everyone had learned one evening not so long ago when they sat down to eat their soup.

The soup had been leek and potato. It had been cooked by Joe's mother for Joe's Dad's boss. She'd been hot and cross for hours in the kitchen preparing a special meal. At last the soup was served. But when Milo coughed up a single, raw potato in the middle of the dining room carpet, the soup spoons went very quiet. Joe's mother's hand had whitened on Milo's collar as she whisked him out of the door.

Poor Milo. Poor Mum. Joe remembered her face when the potato had popped out onto the floor. If she hadn't made such a fuss about it, the dinner would never have been spoiled. But still he wished that Milo would learn what it was that dogs really ate.

"You won't believe what he's done," he complained to his mother in the kitchen. "He's only gone and swallowed my watch while I was in the shower."

"How did he get into the bathroom?"

"Must've left the door open."

"Well then," Joe's Mum said. "What do you expect?"

She was right, Joe thought. It was his own fault for leaving the door open. Everything that happened to you, *you made it happen to yourself.* Or so the book said that had jumped out of the bookcase onto Joe's foot only yesterday. It had only been a paperback, but a heavy one, all the same.

Joe opened the book in surprise. *Face Up To Yourself* – what a title! It was a self-help book that told you *everything was your fault*. Some self-help, Joe thought.

There was no such thing as an accident. You made things fall on your toe. A punch in the eye? Punishment for yourself. A cold? You must have wanted one. Shut your finger in the door? Ouch. Be kinder to yourself next time.

So the time his baggy trousers had been torn off by an escalator, either he or the escalator had meant to do it. It was an odd thought. And the illnesses you could give yourself! Joe read on. The list at the back began with:

Acne: spots show a belief in ugliness. They are little expressions of rage.

And the cure? The healing thought for acne was:

It's safe to have clear skin. I am not angry at all.

Joe ran his hand over his chin. He hoped being angry with Milo wouldn't give him spots. He remembered how angry his mother had been on the day of the dinner party. Milo's dribbly potato had stayed in the middle of the carpet and everyone had tried to ignore it.

The very next day his Dad had turned up for a football match and had sprained his ankle almost at once.

Of course, Joe could see now that his Dad hadn't wanted to play. Fear of failure. It was obvious. He quickly looked up 'sprained ankle' in his book.

Ankle, sprain or break: don't want to walk; poor me; fear of going places.

The healing thought was:

I get around easily. No one is looking at me.

In the next section of the book it said:

You have chosen your parents for exactly the things you need to work on. Value both your parents. You have selected them.

Just then Joe's Dad put his head around the door. "Seen that pesky dog?"

"I selected you," Joe said, holding up the book.

"Huh?"

"I chose you," Joe explained. "It says here: *the parents you have are the parents you deserve.*"

His father squinted at the book. "Milo's sicked up in the hall."

"Did he bring up the car keys you lost?" asked Joe.

"I haven't gone through it yet. I was saving that for a treat."

"Milo can't help it," Joe said.

"You'd think," Joe's Dad said, "you could put things down for a moment. A dog that eats everything. Accidents everywhere."

"It was no accident," Joe said gravely. "It's our fault for having him," Joe said.

His father looked at him closely. "Are you all right, Joe?" he asked.

Chapter 2
Crusties

Tick-tup-tick-tup-tick-tup-tick ... it would drive you mad if you let it. Joe put down the glass.

He had just clamped it onto Milo's belly and it had picked up the sound of his watch ticking away inside. It also picked up the sound of Milo's belly digesting a tin of Turkey 'n' Tripe Meaty Chunks.

It was unbelievable the noise it made: whee-hee-burgle-bup-bup-bup-tigga-liggle-neeee-yor-a-BURK!

You wouldn't believe a belly could make so much noise. It wasn't a pretty sound. Joe's Dad's snoring wasn't pretty either.

It was Sunday afternoon. Time to visit the only person who might possibly be able to help him – Dustin's Dad, Mr Crusty.

Dustin went on the same school bus as Joe. His family lived three streets away. They lived to complain about everything. Dustin's parents went round supermarkets noting mistakes on offers and getting the difference refunded.

The Crusties could get blood out of a stone, Joe's Dad reckoned. And if they could get blood out of a stone, getting a watch out of a dog should be easy.

Mmmm
FREE! FISH WITH EVERY YOGHURT
CLAIM FREE
MULL WORLD
£5 OFF NEXT HAIRCUT
MULL OUR GAME
"GET A FREE TURNIP"
when you buy 50 Turnips
THE GERKIN SHOP
BIG HEDGE HATE
10 TOKENS GETS YOU FREE FLORAL LOO-ROLL COVER
SAVE 4p
TUNNOCK TEA CAKE FAN CLUB
LEAGUE AGAINST BIG HEDGES ASSOCIATION
PANTS
PANTS OFF
would like complain about your shop + the staff who were rude and smelly
Yours
SAVE 3p!
ANGELS
LEATHER

Joe walked round there smartly. He watched Milo carefully at every lamp post he stopped at, but all he did was a wee.

When Joe arrived, Dustin's Dad was in the kitchen making pickle out of nothing but onions, just to prove it could be done.

He spent most of his day working on a court case to force his neighbour to cut his hedge. The hedge, Mr Crusty said, had taken away all his light.

If he had any time left over, Mr Crusty would write letters to the newspaper to complain about other people's letters. The King of Complainers himself had even complained about the Queen.

All that Joe had to do to get Mr Crusty on his side was to choose his words carefully.

"It's Milo," Joe said. "The vet made him swallow my watch."

Mr Crusty went purple. "What's that?" he barked. "Your watch? The vet made Milo *eat* it?"

"Yes," Joe said sadly. "He said it would give him a shadow."

"A shadow? A shadow of what?"

"A shadow on an x-ray. I don't really know," Joe answered.

"That's disgusting!" Mr Crusty leapt out of his seat.

"Isn't it?" Joe said. "It's made him ill already."

Mr Crusty had a dog himself. It was yellow and evil and lived on a smelly blanket on a smelly, yellow settee.

Mr Crusty eyed it fondly.

"We'll give that vet a shadow. We'll give him a *shadow* all right!"

"The thing is, I can't complain until ... "

"Until you have the evidence?"

"Exactly," Joe nodded. Mr Crusty had understood at once.

"Open wide, boy," Mr Crusty said, taking Milo's bad breath full in the face. For a moment his eyes watered. Then he said, "How long has the watch been in there?"

"About a week," Joe lied.

"Simple arithmetic tells me ... "

"Something should have come out?" asked Joe.

"That's why he's ill," said Mr Crusty.

"It must be stuck," Joe agreed.

Mr Crusty brightened. "We must get the evidence out."

Attaboy, Mr Crusty, Joe thought.

Just then Dustin came in. “Not that stupid dog again. Why don’t you tape up his mouth?”

“Why don’t I tape up *yours?*” said Joe.

“If you boys can’t stop scrapping, you’ll have to go outside,” said Mr Crusty.

“Please can you help me?” Joe begged.

Mr Crusty thought about it.

Then he went to his shed. Joe followed slowly. His heart sank when he saw the collection of dusty old bottles that sat on the shelves. Was this such a good idea? What had he let Milo in for?

“I’m not that desperate,” he said. “Really, I think I’ll just wait.”

LUMP CREAM
EXTRA STRONG
moist spice
Parsnip Fudge
SUPERFROTH
JAM 1999
EXTRACT OF FISH
LEG GEL
BOIL HELP
PUKE Juice
Tart Pickle
LEMON 1975 CURD
BLACK GOOIE STUFF

"Nonsense, there must be a blockage." Mr Crusty took out a spoon. He took down a sticky, brown bottle and briskly tried to open it until the veins stood out on his head.

"Really, it doesn't matter," Joe began.

"Won't be a minute. Hang on."

Joe hung on while Mr Crusty ran the bottle under the hot tap and gripped it with a tea towel. The veins on his neck looked like ropes.

Joe thought Mr Crusty's head would burst. "I don't think it's going to open," Joe said.

Mr Crusty let out a sudden hiss between his teeth that made Milo sneeze three times. Even his ears were red. Mr Crusty's ears, that is, not Milo's.

Joe hung on while Mr Crusty doused the bottle with oil. He hung on while he fetched the pliers and destroyed the screw-on cap. Then, still hanging on, Joe followed Mr Crusty down to the field, where he put the bottle on a stump.

"Shoot the top off. Wonderful stuff. Have it open in no time."

Mr Crusty fired his air gun. In no time he'd used up his pellets. Still the bottle stood there. Purple with rage, Mr Crusty pelted it with stones. But every stone missed its mark.

With a sudden, wild cry, he rushed at the bottle and jumped on it.

"We've got to go now," Joe said. "Milo wants to get back."

Mr Crusty ignored him. "Marvellous stuff! Acts on the bowels like dynamite! Fix your dog in a jiffy!"

Joe and Milo escaped.

"Wonderful stuff!" Mr Crusty roared after them. They could hear him from two streets away.

Joe walked briskly home. Milo looked up at him gratefully. Did he know he'd had a lucky escape?

It was then that the funny thing happened.

Though of course, it was no accident.

Chapter 3
Time Out

Something came bowling down the road. Joe picked it up. An orange. Something made him close his eyes. A line or two from *Face Up To Yourself* ran over and over in his head:

I am free and unafraid. I choose good things now.

A woman came after the orange. “Oh,” she said, “you’ve found it.”

Joe handed it back. “Yes,” he said. Her hair was orange too. “You’re going to drop some more,” he said, “if you don’t fix the hole in your basket.”

“Oh.” She laughed and looked down. “The animals won’t like it if everything drops out.”

He saw she had carrots and lettuce, bananas, apples, grapes. “Animals?”

“Come and see, if you like. I only live round the corner.”

Joe wasn’t sure if he should.

“I’m Ria,” she said. “Andy’s sister.”

“Oh.” Joe remembered Andy. “But he moved away, didn’t he?”

Ria nodded. “But I stayed on. I’ve been studying you see.”

“I’m Joe.”

“I know,” Ria smiled. “What’s the time?” she asked.

“Ask Milo. He swallowed my watch.”

“What’s the time, Milo?” Ria said.

The clock on the corner shop said 2:52, but Milo didn’t know about that. He knew a lot about Ria though. She smelled good. She looked good. He would follow Ria to the ends of the earth. Instead he followed her home.

“I’m going off to Borneo,” said Ria, as if she had read Milo’s thoughts.

“Where’s Borneo?”

"The South China Sea's to the north," she told him, pointing it out on the map on the wall of her room. "Java and Sumatra to the south ... "

"*Borneo?*" Joe interrupted. "Why would you want to go there?"

"Because I'm a witch," she said.

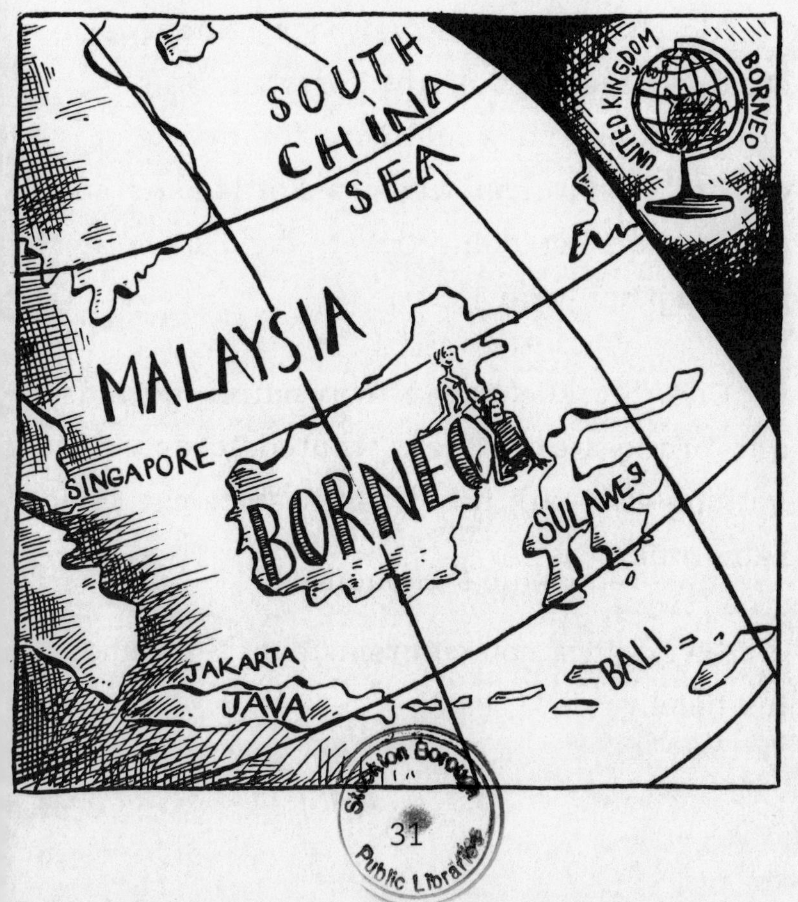

Joe stared at her in surprise.

"That's what I'll be, when I get there. A witch with bright red hair."

How unusual she was. How special she'd look to people who had never seen her before. They wouldn't know she was a vet.

Ria showed Joe her vet books. She was studying the apes of the forest. It was orang-utans she would care for at the animal hospital in western Borneo. As soon as she had her plane ticket, she'd be winging her way there.

One day she hoped to research gorillas and orang-utans. She'd wanted to do nothing else with her life ever since she could remember.

"Ever since you can remember?" Joe shook his head.

Then he saw something move in a box by the heater. He peered in and saw three baby hedgehogs.

"They have to be fed every hour," Ria said. "Their mother died on the road." She handed him an eye dropper full of milk and showed him what to do. How funny she was with her red hair the colour of the orang-utan fur on the poster behind her.

"How many's left?" Joe said.

"How many what?" asked Ria.

"Orang-utans."

"About 27,000."

"Those are all the orang-utans in the whole *world?*" Joe gaped. "Anyway, how do they know?"

"Because people like me go and count them."

"You'd better be careful," Joe said. "Out there in the jungle."

"I've had my injections already."

"There's leeches. And snakes," Joe said seriously. "A tree might fall on your head."

"It might not," said ape doctor Ria.

"You want to be careful," Joe said. "There's accidents everywhere."

It was no accident that the rabbit escaped.

Ria's rabbits lived in a hutch at the bottom of her garden. Joe enjoyed petting them, especially a whopper named Bugsy. He took her out and stroked her.

Accidentally-on-purpose, he let her go. In moments, she had wriggled through the fence and was off across the park.

They chased her breathlessly around the duckpond and through the Swan Café. Finally they cornered her in the miniature train. Poor Bugsy was terrified.

Ria showed Joe how to calm her. She was very calm herself.

"Ice cream?" she offered.

Joe looked at Bugsy. "You take her home. I'll get them."

Joe went up to the ice cream kiosk at the side of the Swan Café. He looked at the choice. Tangle Twister? Mivvy? Double-choc Fiesta? He decided Ria would probably go for a lemon 'n' lime Monkey Business.

"Nice," Ria said, when she came back.

Joe was glad he'd guessed right. It was no accident that they played endlessly in the park with Milo and a frisbee until at last Joe covered his mouth with his hand. "I've got to go," he said. "It must be very late."

He never knew what time it was, now. It was funny. He liked it that way.

The game in the park had seemed timeless, with the tea-time sun lighting up Ria's red hair and setting on the last games of soccer. He must have meant to lose his watch. He didn't miss it at all.

He walked home with Ria and stopped by her house. You wouldn't need watches in Borneo, Joe thought. Probably monkeys would eat them or mists would stop the clocks. It rained a lot in Borneo. It would probably rot your socks.

"Nice to meet you, Milo." Ria covered Milo's eyes with his ears. Milo slobbered over her hands. He loved her to death, Joe could see.

"Watch his motions, won't you?" she said to Joe. She saw that he was puzzled.

Joe nodded, mystified.

"Yeah," he said. "I'll watch 'em."

She waved her long, explorer's arm in a long, explorer's goodbye.

Joe would find out for himself that motions were just Milo's poo.

"Bye, Joe. Bye, Milo. Come and see me if nothing moves."

Joe watched Milo lope home. His motions looked fine. What did she mean? Was it the way he walked?

Chapter 4
Titus

At four o'clock the next day, they went to the zoo. It seeemed incredible, but they did it. Ria came round in her van. She spoke to Joe's Mum for five minutes. Then they were on their way.

They reached the zoo at a quarter past four, which meant that they had just over an hour to look round before closing time. Ria

often helped out at the zoo. So they both got in for free.

"I've got something to show you," she winked, racing Joe to the Ape House.

There were three gorillas in the compound. Richard and Samson were huge, but Titus was really something. He was always the boss of the others. Joe laughed when Ria showed him how Richard annoyed Titus by rattling a door in their compound. Titus would rush over to threaten him. Then Richard would dash outside with Titus hot on his heels. Seconds later Richard would coolly pop in again to start a game with Samson.

Joe pressed his face to the reinforced glass. The compound had platforms and ropes, nets and tyres and straw. The gorillas had a whole island outside.

"As good an environment," Ria had said, "as captive apes could have."

Richard and Samson played tag. Suddenly Titus charged in, skidding across the floor like a giant school inspector. He glared around him with a fierce expression. *Ay-oy. Wot's all this*?

At once, Richard and Samson pretended they were unravelling ropes or picking the rims of their tyres.

Joe and Ria laughed. They watched it again and again. The door rattling; the chasing outside; Titus's sudden charge; Richard and Samson's game. Ria explained that this was dominance behaviour.

They looked into the next door compound. There was a mother orang-utan in there with her baby.

The mother sat in a corner piling straw on her head. The baby hung from a net with its spidery arms like pipe cleaners. Joe watched the keeper feeding them a drink out of a bottle.

"Looks like Ribena," he laughed.

They watched the apes for a long time. Then they had to go.

They went back past the gorillas, where Richard and Samson were looking guilty. Joe searched for Titus – where had he got to now?

Suddenly they saw him, swinging feet-first straight at them!

With a terrific bang on the glass, Titus dropped into a net.

Joe went a little pale. "Good job that glass is strong!"

"It's his party trick," Ria said. "Titus weighs twenty stone."

Joe looked at Titus. Twenty stone. Titus eyed Joe closely. He knew the effect he made, crashing into the glass. He knew how to terrify Richard and Samson. *Don't forget who's boss*, said his terrifyingly human eyes.

"And you're going to look after *these* guys?" Joe turned to Ria, astonished.

"They're hunted. Starved. Lost and confused. Why wouldn't I?" Ria told him.

Joe bought an orang-utan soft toy in the shop and a stick of rock for Ria. She would need to be a rock of courage to put up with everything in Borneo. Malaria, insects, leeches. Constant mud and heat.

Where did you order courage? Some catalogue, perhaps?

He remembered Titus's tiny eye; the human-like intelligence in it.

The map on the wall of the Ape House had shown up only three small areas where orang-utans still survived; only one where gorillas still lived.

Help us, Titus might have said, with the bang of his feet on the glass. *Look at me! How mighty I am! Still my people are dying!*

The red witch had heard his cry. It was no accident, Joe thought, that Ria was a special person.

Chapter 5
Night Kitchen

Joe's mother wasn't expecting him. "What – back already?"

Joe took a breath.

"It was brilliant. Titus, he's the boss, he swings at the glass with his feet. And there's this baby orang-utan. Its mother puts straw on her head, and the keeper, he feeds them Ribena."

"Has Ria gone?"

"Yes," Joe said, "she had to get back. She's going to Borneo soon."

"But it's only half past four. How could you have gone to the zoo and back in less than half an hour?"

For a moment, Joe looked puzzled. "I don't know," he said, "but we did. And there's lions there, and tigers, and Ria goes in for free ... "

Joe's mother looked at him. "Mr Crusty sent round a bottle of goo. I don't know what you want done with it."

So he'd finally got it open. Joe smelled it. Disgusting. "It's for Milo," he said.

I've been to the zoo with a witch, he thought. *A red witch who looks after apes.*

"I should think," his mother said, "you've got as much chance of getting that stuff down Milo as getting him on *Ready, Steady, Cook.*"

Joe felt cross. He *might* get Milo on telly one day. Who was to say he wouldn't? "Bet you don't know where Borneo is," he yelled, looking it up on the Internet.

"Part of Malaysia, isn't it?"

Joe double-clicked on 'primates'. "How do you spell orang-utan?"

His mother spelled it out and Joe keyed it in. His search had narrowed down a bit.

He found the Animal Hospital in Borneo. There were pictures, 'Orang-utans Rescued This Year'. There was even a family tree to show how the apes were related.

BORNEO
ANIMAL HOSPITAL
THE COUNTRY
MONKEY WORLD
TRAVEL
BORNEO

Joe hadn't realised how much there was to be done or how many people were doing it. The founder of the Animal Hospital grinned out of the screen wearing three or four apes round her neck.

Joe went deeper, further. He could practically *hear* the jungle ... even in bed he could hear it ...

****

That night Milo got bored. The moonlight came in on the kitchen floor and shone into his basket. He got up and padded around. He ate a few biscuits he didn't want. Then he flopped down again.

After a while he got an itch. He got up and scratched it thoroughly, his foot bang-banging on the floor.

He played with a spider which ran out from under the fridge. It made him sneeze quite a lot. But he ate it anyway.

Then he got an itch on his back and blundered around the table a bit to scratch himself on the legs. Something fell over. A bottle. A stream of gummy-looking, brown stuff dripped off the edge of the table and collected in a pool on the floor.

Milo licked it. It tasted of fish, strange roots, liquorice, rust and indescribable flavours.

With his big, pink, floppy tongue, Milo licked up the rest of it ...

Chapter 6
Milo's Revenge

Milo usually waited at the bus stop with Joe.

The school bus would come and Milo would pad sadly home. Joe had got used to his miserable expression by now. But still, he looked sadder than usual this morning.

Dustin stood beside him, but a million miles away. Dustin belonged to the 'hard'

BUS STOP

gang who never spoke to anyone outside the 'click'. That was what his mother called it. "Don't mind them. It's a click."

She meant they were a group who didn't want any outsiders, which was exactly what they were. They hardly spoke to each other in case somebody took the mickey. Joe always tried to say nothing. That way you were reasonably safe.

Right now they were laughing at Milo. Just because he'd burped.

"Dogs don't burp."

"This one does."

"Dumb-looking dog," Dustin said. He stepped on the end of Milo's tail. Milo looked up at him dolefully.

Dustin increased the pressure. Milo sneezed and got up. His good nature wouldn't let him see that Dustin had done it on purpose. Still Joe seethed inside.

"Leave it, Joe," someone said.

Dustin's bag lay half-open behind him as he stuffed down his ration of sweets. Flumps, crisps, Kit Kats, Snickers, Treats, Rollos, Nerds, Fizzas, Wispas and even stale pies from the factory his mother worked at. Dustin would eat anything.

"All right, then, Dustin Dustbin?" Joe suddenly said. "That would be breakfast, then, would it?"

Dustin crammed in a Mars bar and wiped his mouth. Then he went into action. He tore Joe's bag off his back and threw it to Jason. Jason threw it to Simon. Simon chucked it to Tom. Tom chucked it over the fence.

"Thanks," Joe said. "Nice."

He would have to climb over the fence to get it. Now his heart was hammering.

They snatched off his shoe as he went. By the time he'd rescued his bag, his shoe was propping up a traffic sign in the middle of two lanes of rush-hour traffic.

Now the bus was coming. Joe felt he was falling to pieces as he dodged out into the traffic.

Got it. He waved his shoe in triumph. Now to get back.

But something was happening at the bus stop. Something revolting.

Something to do with Milo.

"Ergh! No! That's *sick!*" Dustin was doing a dance of disgust.

"You getting on, or what?" The bus driver wasn't sympathetic.

Dustin had to sit on his own. No one would even go near him.

Milo padded home and slept the rest of the day. It hadn't been Milo's fault. The mixture he'd drunk had done its work, just rather suddenly, that was all.

"Ur-ur-*urrgh!*" Dustin heaved. But he had to take it to school. He had to try to wash it out. To be called the dump-truck all day. To sit in class, ignored. And all because of his Dad's dynamite mixture. And what Milo had done in his bag.

Chapter 7
I'll Sue

"But something good came out of it," Joe explained to his Mum when he came home. "The cleaner found my watch in the cloakroom. Dustin must have found it in his bag, you know, when Milo ... "

"I don't want to hear about it," his mother said.

It was really revolting. Dog poo in Dustin's bag.

"Good old Milo," Joe said.

Suddenly he looked puzzled. 2:52, his watch had said, when the cleaner had handed it back.

"That's funny," he said.

"What?" his Mum wanted to know.

"Nothing," Joe said, but he had thought of something.

2:52. He remembered the time on the corner shop clock just before they'd hurried back with Ria to feed the baby hedgehogs. His watch must have stopped in Milo's insides at the *exact moment that he'd met the red witch.* Ria had stopped all the clocks. He guessed she *was* really magic.

That night Joe helped plant runner beans. His Dad made the holes. Joe dropped a bean in each hole.

Then suddenly Mr Crusty appeared.

“Hey you!” he roared over the bean poles, as soon as he sighted the top of Joe’s Dad’s head.

“What can I do for you, sir?” Joe’s Dad leaned on his spade. “Here comes trouble,” he added under his breath.

“Buy a new school bag, for starters.” Mr Crusty had a point. Dustin’s bag smelled and looked crappy, which is just what it was. “I believe your dog had an accident.” Mr Crusty looked furious.

“After Dustin stood on his *tail*,” Joe protested.

"There was some bullying," Joe's Dad said.

Mr Crusty narrowed his eyes. "What's that got to do with anything?"

Joe's Dad picked up a sticky, brown bottle and handed it to Mr Crusty. "While we're at it, have this back."

"That dog wants putting down," Mr Crusty insisted.

"It's your own fault," Joe lashed back. "It was your stupid medicine that did it."

Mr Crusty shook with rage. "I want a new bag out of you!"

"All right, all right." Joe's Dad handed Mr Crusty a tenner. Then he snatched it back again. "Thank you, sir," he said. "Your contribution towards cleaning our carpets is very welcome. You didn't mean to poison our dog ... "

"P – poison?" Mr Crusty stammered.

"I don't know what you did to him, but it could have been really serious."

"Actually, I think he drank too much ... " Joe felt he had to say. But nothing could stop his Dad now.

"It's not wise to dose people's dogs unless you know what you're doing. Joe could sue you, you know."

Joe watched Mr Crusty anxiously. He had gone very red.

"People should be warned. I might even write to the paper." Joe's Dad was laughing, now. "A letter to the RSPCA ... "

"No need for that," Mr Crusty blurted out. He turned and walked off down the path, trailing brown, sticky liquid from his bottle over the cracks filled with dandelions and daisies.

The daisies wilted; the dandelions steamed.

How had Milo drunk it?

"Thanks," Joe's Dad said. "The path needed weeding. Any time you're passing."

Chapter 8
Start the Clock

Indoors, over tea, Joe put on Mr Crusty's face until everyone was tired of laughing. Milo chased his tail. He knew when something was funny. Finally they got on with pudding.

"So Milo's been a bit like the crocodile," said Joe's Mum.

"What crocodile?" Joe looked blank.

"The crocodile in *Hook*, of course. He swallowed a clock. That's how you knew he was coming."

"It's been more than that," Joe told her. Milo and the watch had just been part of it. But still there was something else. Ria. The game in the park. The trip to the zoo and back in *less than half an hour.*

Somehow he had had 'time out' from being Joe. He had been in Ria's world. Now that he was back in his own world again, he'd better account for his time. Every minute counted. How had he not known before?

He brought out his watch, now cleaned. For the first time since he'd got it back he felt the need to re-set it. He showed it to his mother.

"You see? Still stuck at 2:52, the *exact time* I … "

"You what?"

But Joe felt suddenly shy. Too late to explain the magic that went with Ria. Even if it was true that the watch had stopped when he met her. "The exact time Milo swallowed it, of course. Remember?"

"How could I forget?" Mum said.

"What a family," his Dad groaned.

"What a dog," Joe agreed. He could see that they blamed themselves. "It's not your fault these things happen," Joe said, even though it was. "You shouldn't care what people think. You're excellent parents," he said.

"Thank you," his Dad said. "We know."

N
E
W
R

Chapter 9

I Choose Good Things Now

When Joe revisited Ria's place on a golden summer evening some two weeks later, he didn't know what to expect.

What he found was an empty house with a swinging gate. She'd gone. So soon.

He'd only just got to know her. Couldn't she have stayed a bit longer? He dragged his feet to the door. If only she were behind it. The letter box showed him a square of blank hall. Had she released the hedgehogs? Yes. He could picture her now. Probably in the moonlight. Probably deep in the woodland, the night before she left.

Then she'd boarded her flight and winged her way to Borneo, looking forward only, never behind her.

Yet he couldn't blame her. She'd wanted to go – ever since she could remember. And now she'd finally gone.

The rabbit hutches hung open. It was as if she'd never been there. Had she been real, he wondered?

Then he spotted the gorilla poster still looking down at him from her newly emptied room.

And he knew that somewhere out in the jungle, her long arm parted leaves. Spidery orang-utan babies clung to her neck and their bright eyes looked out of her hair. She cared for them when the loggers had cut down the trees and their parents had starved to death.

She would become a legend, the red witch. So gentle. So caring. So strong. Trees would fall, but not on her. Fabulously spotted snakes would watch her every move. Still she'd be safe, he knew. She was exactly where she wanted to be. Doing what she wanted to do.

Making her own life happen.

Joe climbed into her garden and latched up an empty hutch. A long wisp of red hair was caught in its wire. He took it out and it blew away on the wind and out over the park and away.

Oranges. Red hair. Orang-utans. The red witch of western Borneo. How had she come into his life? Somehow *he'd* brought her into it. When she'd chased that orange.

Joe remembered that silly book. *Face Up To Yourself.* No accidents. No excuses. He looked at his newly-set watch. It was going again. Already the minutes were ticking away. How would his own life happen?

He could read, act, travel, sing, study, climb, fish, think, paint, build, race, sculpt, fight, dance, drive, dive, fly. He could do anything he wanted to do. He'd start by visiting Mr Crusty. It hadn't been Mr Crusty's fault. He'd tried to help. It had all gone wrong.

Joe went home. It was no accident that the unopened bottle of Victorian Pickle almost fell into his hand when he opened the cupboard. Just the ticket, as Mr Crusty would say. He knew Mr Crusty would like it.

With the pickle in his hand, Joe set out to the Crusties. Mr Crusty wasn't so bad. Even Dustin was all right, if you got him alone, that was.

In no time, Joe had rounded the corner. Down the street stood Crusty World, overshadowed by its neighbour's hedge. An evil-looking yellow dog waited to bite Joe's ankle.

Joe shook his head. He knocked on the door. No excuses. He wondered if they'd be in.

Other Barrington Stoke titles available:

What's Going On, Gus? by Jill Atkins 1-902260-10-4
Nicked! by David Belbin 1-902260-29-5
Bungee Hero by Julie Bertagna 1-902260-23-6
Hostage by Malorie Blackman 1-902260-12-0
The Two Jacks by Tony Bradman 1-902260-30-9
Starship Rescue by Theresa Breslin 1-902260-24-4
Ghost for Sale by Terry Deary 1-902260-14-7
Sam the Detective by Terrance Dicks 1-902260-19-8
Billy the Squid by Colin Dowland 1-902260-04-X
Eddie and the Zedlines by Colin Dowland 1-902260-31-7
Kick Back by Vivian French 1-902260-02-3
The Gingerbread House by Adèle Geras 1-902260-03-1
Danny's Great Goal by Michael Hardcastle 1-902260-32-5
Ship of Ghosts by Nigel Hinton 1-902260-33-3
Virtual Friend by Mary Hoffman 1-902260-00-7
The Genie by Mary Hooper 1-902260-20-1
Picking on Percy by Cathy MacPhail 1-902260-44-9
Tod in Biker City by Anthony Masters 1-902260-15-5
Wartman by Michael Morpurgo 1-902260-05-8
Who's a Big Bully Then by Michael Morpurgo 1-902260-43-0
Whirlwind by Judith O'Neill 1-902260-34-1
Extra Time by Jenny Oldfield 1-902260-13-9
Screw Loose by Alison Prince 1-902260-01-5
Second Chance by Alison Prince 1-902260-46-5
Life Line by Rosie Rushton 1-902260-21-X
Problems with a Python by Jeremy Strong 1-902260-22-8
Lift Off by Hazel Townson 1-902260-11-2

Barrington Stoke would like to thank all its readers for commenting on the manuscript before publication and in particular:

Louise Black
Kate Hamilton-Bowker
Sarah Evans
Stuart Kane
Marc Kenney
Jonathan MacDonald
Dauntie Muirhead

Barrington Stoke Club

Would you like to become a member of our club? Children who write to us with their views become members of our club and special advisors to the company. They also have the chance to act as editors on future manuscripts. Contact us at the address or website below – we'd love to hear from you!

Barrington Stoke, 10 Belford Terrace, Edinburgh EH4 3DQ
Tel: 0131 315 4933 Fax: 0131 315 4934
E-mail: info@barringtonstoke.co.uk
Website: www.barringtonstoke.co.uk